JOHNNY
LONG LEGS

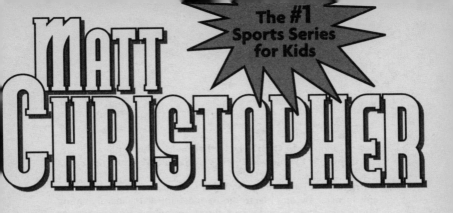

The #1
Sports Series
for Kids

MATT CHRISTOPHER

JOHNNY
LONG LEGS

Little, Brown and Company
Boston   New York   London

First Edition

Matt Christopher™ is a trademark of Catherine M. Christopher

Library of Congress Cataloging-in-Publicaton Data

Christopher; Matt.
    Johnny Long Legs, by Matt Christopher.
        p.   cm.
    ISBN 0-316-14065-1
    Summary: Even though he is the tallest member of the bas-
ketball team, a young boy finds he is far from being the best
player.
    [1. Basketball — Fiction.]   I. Title
PZ7.C458Jo [Fic]   78-113437 AC

20 19 18

COM-MO

Printed in the United States of America

To my cousin, Fred

JOHNNY
LONG LEGS

1

"Come on, Johnny," said Toby, brown-haired, a head shorter and on the stocky side. "Let's get the toboggan."

Johnny Reese pushed aside the thoughts of the home he and Mom had left in New York City and followed his new, younger brother to the garage where a long, pale blue toboggan was hung on the wall. The boys lifted it off the hook and set it on the floor.

Man, though Johnny. *A* toboggan. *A sled. An aquarium in the living room. What is it*

*that this stepbrother of mine doesn't have?
Back in the city I had nothing.*

"You'd be a good man on our basketball team, Johnny," observed Toby, smiling. "We need a guy with long legs."

Johnny grinned and pulled his hat down over his ears. The early December air was nippy. "You play basketball in this small town?"

"What do you mean?" snapped Toby. "Sure we do. We have a Junior Basketball League and play twice a week. We've already played two games."

A league? Man! He had never played in a league game. Just scrub.

The boys pulled the toboggan across the snow-packed road to the hill, climbed all the way to the top of it, and then rode down, Johnny sitting behind Toby. The wind lashed against their faces, the sound of the runners sang in their ears.

2

The field was long. The boys coasted nearly to the edge of it, close to the fence, and then started to pull the toboggan back up again. One hundred feet away two guys were cruising along briskly on a snowmobile.

"Am I glad my dad and your mom got married," said Toby. "I was getting tired of Grandpa's cooking. Potatoes, hamburg, and hot dogs. You get tired of that after a while."

"I suppose," said Johnny, thoughtfully.

He had lost his dad in a car accident and Toby's mother had died from an illness. Later Johnny's mother and Toby's father had met at an education convention in New York City and had written each other ever since.

Then along came the letter from Toby's father asking Mom to marry him. It seemed to be the happiest moment in Mom's life. Johnny didn't know what to think of it at first. But after a long talk with Mom she convinced him that she really loved the guy. And she'd been pretty lonely since Johnny's dad had died. In the end, Johnny was glad she'd met Mr. Reese.

"I hope you won't mind living in a small town," Mr. Reese had written. "You can put Lansburg on two blocks in New York City and still have room to spare."

Of course she didn't mind it a single bit. And Johnny didn't think he would either.

A thin spiral of smoke curled up from the snowy ground ahead of them. Johnny stooped, squashed the burning tip of a cigarette into the snow, then stood and rubbed it clean.

"What are you going to do with that?" asked Toby curiously.

"Smoke it," said Johnny. "Back home us guys . . ." He paused and looked at Toby. "Why?"

"Does Mom know you smoke?"

"No. But I don't much, anyway."

"Better not let Dad see you," warned Toby.

"You going to snitch?"

Toby didn't answer for a minute. "No," he said then.

Johnny unzipped a coat pocket and dropped the butt into it. "Come on," he said. "Let's get up the hill."

He started school on Monday. Mom drove him there. He handed his transfer papers from Public School No. 14 to Mr. Taylor, the guidance counselor, who introduced him to his new homeroom teacher, Miss Abby. She was shorter than Johnny in spite of her high heels and wore her black hair up high.

Miss Abby introduced him to the class, then requested one of the boys, a Jim Sain, to show Johnny to his classes after each period. She gave Johnny a card on which were listed the subjects he was going to take, the room numbers, and the hours.

Jim Sain was slightly shorter than Johnny and reminded him of some of the boys at P.S. 14. His black uncombed hair hung over his ears. His clothes were disheveled, as if he had slept in them. His face looked waxen, as if it seldom cracked a smile.

After the period was over, a finger jabbed Johnny's shoulder. "Come on," said Jim Sain. "Grab your English book."

Johnny followed him to a classroom down the hall. Students passed back and forth in the hallway in droves, their arms loaded with books. Boys greeted Jim and looked at Johnny appraisingly.

Johnny saw Toby and for the first time felt like smiling. "Hi, Toby."

"Hi, Johnny. How are you doing? Hi, Jim."

"Hi," said Jim.

Johnny wanted to stop a moment and talk with his stepbrother. But Jim kept walking and Johnny didn't have a chance to. *What's the matter with the guy?* Johnny asked himself. *Is it my fault that Miss Abby asked him to show me to my classes?*

At lunchtime, twelve-fifteen, the two boys walked down the long white corridor to the cafeteria.

"You stand in line here to buy lunch," grunted Jim.

Johnny looked around for Toby. "When do the seventh graders eat?" he asked.

"They already have," answered Jim. "We're the last ones." He looked at Johnny and chuckled. "That makes us big shots, I guess."

They got their lunches and carried them to the long tables. Johnny started to follow Jim, then paused when Jim put his tray on the table and sat between two boys. The next vacant place was five chairs away. Johnny went to it, placed his tray on the table, and sat down.

Several girls sitting across from him were talking in soft tones and laughing, and for a minute he wondered whether they were laughing at him. After a while he realized they were talking about some girl's hair style.

"Are you Toby's cousin?" asked the boy next to him.

"Stepbrother," said Johnny.

"I'm Bert Buttons," said the boy. He had a mop of blond hair and lots of freckles. "Guys call me Stitch."

He held out a hand and Johnny took it.

"Stitch, huh?" Johnny grinned. "I'm Johnny Reese."

"I've never seen you before."

"Came Saturday," said Johnny.

8

"From where?"

"New York City."

He lifted his glass of milk. Just as he started to drink it someone bumped his head and half of the milk spilled over his shirtfront and pants.

"Oh! Sorry!"

Johnny looked around. Jim Sain was standing there, a faint, apologetic smile on his face.

Instant anger flashed in Johnny's eyes. He felt like belting Jim, but he controlled himself and didn't move.

"What happened?" asked a sharp, adult voice.

Johnny saw a man in a black suit and green tie looking at them from the next table.

"I bumped into him," confessed Jim. "And the milk spilled on his shirt."

Johnny wiped the milk from his clothes with a napkin. Jim might have bumped him by accident but there was a lot of room between the chairs. And the way Jim had been acting toward him . . .

"I saw it happen," said one of the girls. "Jim did it on purpose."

"I did not!" Jim snarled. "Anyway, who asked for your two cents?"

He suddenly swung off to the kitchen with his tray, then stamped out of the cafeteria with long, bold strides.

Johnny looked at the girl. Her brown eyes matched her thick shoulder-length hair. "Are you sure he did it on purpose?"

"Yes, I'm sure. If I were you I'd knock his block off."

"Enough of that, Karen." The man in the black suit had come over and was standing behind Johnny. "I'll speak to Jim about this," he said. "You're the new boy, aren't you? Johnny Reese?"

"Yes. But you don't have to speak to him, sir. It could have been an accident."

"I'll speak to him anyway." The man smiled, patted Johnny on the shoulder, and left.

"That's Mr. Thomas," said Stitch. "He'll speak to Jim, but I doubt if it'll do any good."

"He's a punk," said the girl.

Johnny finished his lunch, feeling better now that someone had come on his side. Jim was a strange one, all right. His type was the last Johnny had expected to see here in Lansburg.

"Do you play basketball?" asked Stitch.

"Some," replied Johnny.

"Maybe you can play with us. We're the White Cats. Toby's on our team. You might have your chance to get even with Jim on the court. He plays with the Hornets."

Johnny felt discouraged. He didn't want to get even with anyone. He had hoped not to make enemies here. Especially not on the first day of school.

2

On Tuesday, December 7, the White Cats played the Swordtails at five o'clock in the Community Hall gymnasium. Tonight was the third night of the Junior Basketball League. The White Cats' record was one win, one loss.

Toby introduced Johnny to Coach Biff Dates, a big, barrel-chested man. AUBURN was printed on the back of his sweatshirt.

"Can we use him?" Toby asked. "He played basketball a lot in New York City."

"In that case I think we can," answered the coach, pumping Johnny's hand and looking him up and down with a very pleased expression on his round face. "We need those long legs. Did you play center, Johnny?"

"Mostly." Johnny blushed. Everybody always reminded him of his long legs.

"Well, that's where I would put you," said the coach. "Can't try you out tonight anyway. Have to register you first. I'll watch you work out tomorrow night and possibly start you Thursday against the Astro Jets."

Coach Dates introduced him to the members of the team and let him sit on the bench with them. The White Cats uniform was all white with the team's name printed on the front and numbers on the back. Toby's number was 8. He played left guard. The other guard was Cotton Cornish. At center was Rick Davis. The forwards were Stitch Buttons and Huck Stevens.

Johnny couldn't get over the large, beautiful gym. The two baskets had glass backboards behind them. A large electric score-board was at one end. A movable seating stand was against one wall. This court would put the one he had played on in New York to shame.

And imagine having a ref with a black and white striped shirt and black pants with white stripes down the sides. The kids in his neighborhood never had real refs. They took turns refereeing themselves.

Rick scored the first basket with a layup, then Toby tossed one in from a corner to put the White Cats in a 4 to 0 lead. Later the referee's whistle shrilled and a foul was called on Huck. Huck had struck a Swordtail's hand when the player jumped for a layup.

Two shots. The Swordtail missed the first and made the second.

Gradually the Swordtails crept ahead of the White Cats. The Cats finally evened the score, rallied for a while, then fell behind again. They trailed 12 to 10 when the first quarter ended.

Then Johnny realized that he was alone on the bench. The other players were standing around Coach Biff Dates. No one seemed to notice him and he didn't know whether to join them or not. He stayed there.

I don't know, he thought. *I never played basketball like it's played here. Move your foot an inch and you're called for traveling. Touch a guy and it's a foul. I've never played by such strict rules.*

There were basketball leagues in New York City but Mom had not wanted him to join a team. She had not wanted him to play basketball at all. Only after he had pleaded with her had she allowed him to play scrub games. She didn't care for basketball. She didn't care at all for athletics.

Was it his fault that he had to prove to the guys that he was no sissy by smoking with them? Once a kid had dared him to swipe a melon from a fruit stand. He swiped it, but had been caught and made to promise he would never steal again or he'd go to jail. He had kept that promise.

The second quarter got under way. Huck dumped in three field goals himself. The quarter ended with the Swordtails leading, 26 to 23.

The White Cats fell further behind in the third quarter. Then Cotton Cornish got hot in the fourth and sank three in a row, plus a foul shot. Rick laid in a couple and Toby sank two long ones to put the White Cats back in the lead.

When the final whistle blew the Cats won by two points, 61 to 59.

"Told you we have a good fighting club," said Toby, dressing in the locker room after a quick shower. "When Thursday comes we'll be even better."

Johnny would be on the team then. He felt tense and worried, though. Toby believed that he was a darn good basketball player just because he was tall. But he wasn't. Toby and the whole White Cats team were going to be in for a real disappointment.

He practiced with the White Cats the next evening. In a scrimmage game Coach Dates played him at center and he just barely out-jumped his opponent, a kid much shorter than he. He wondered whether the coach would put him in at all in the White Cats' next game.

The coach gave him a uniform before the Astro Jets game which meant, at least, that he was on the White Cats' team. Number 4 was on the back of the jersey.

"Biggest size I have," the coach said, smiling.

Johnny stood in line with the other players before the game started and shot baskets with them. He felt everyone's eyes on him, watching to see how well he performed. He was the tallest boy on the team, topping Rick by an inch.

The game started. Both teams seemed evenly matched. The first quarter was half over when Coach Dates nudged Johnny. "Go in for Rick, Johnny. Report to the score-keeper."

Johnny shook his opponent's hand as he had seen the players do, then hopped around the center of the court, waiting for Toby to throw the ball in from out of bounds.

Toby passed it to him. He caught it, dribbled across the center line, and then stopped as an Astro Jet tried to pounce on the ball. Johnny lifted it high out of the way, then pivoted.

The whistle shrilled.

"Traveling!" cried the ref, twirling his hands to show the infraction.

Johnny stared at him. Traveling? He had barely moved his foot!

The Astro Jets took out the ball. Huck intercepted the pass-in, dribbled a few steps, then passed to Johnny. Johnny drove in for a layup, but a hand rose in front of him and tapped the ball away.

An enthusiastic yell came from the Astro Jet fans. Bewildered, Johnny looked at the player who had stopped him from making a basket. A boy at least a foot shorter than he!

"Way to jump, Stogy!" yelled a fan.

The Astro Jets had the ball and were taking it down their end of the court. An instant later an Astro Jet passed. Another caught the ball, leaped, and sank it for two points.

Toby ran upcourt and met Johnny's eyes. A stunned look was on his face.

"Thought you had one for sure," he said disappointedly.

3

Johnny learned that the small Astro Jet who had outjumped him was Stogy Giles. For each basket scored by one of his teammates, Stogy scored two. He was lightning fast and easily the best player on the Astro Jets team.

Johnny stayed in when the second quarter started. The Astro Jets were leading 13 to 7. They took the ball from out of bounds and moved it across the court in a series of quick, snappy passes. Johnny covered the backboard as an Astro Jet shot one from the foul line, but an Astro Jet outjumped him and caught the rebound.

A yell went up from the Astro Jet fans. "Nice going, Stogy! Those long legs! They're too heavy for him to lift!"

Johnny tried to shut out the needling cries. They pricked and hurt. *Could he help it that he couldn't jump? He was trying, wasn't he?*

Nat Newton took Toby's place and plunked one in from a corner. Later Johnny was fouled as he tried a layup and was given two shots. While he bounced the ball at the foul line he prayed he would make both of them. Making both would help to cancel out his poor jumping.

He hit the first shot and missed the second.

He rushed in for the rebound. But once again Stogy Giles outjumped him and took possession of the ball for the Astro Jets.

He scooted under Johnny's outstretched arm like a bug, dribbled all the way down-court, then shot a pass to a teammate. The Jet broke for the basket and scored.

The quarter was half over when Coach Dates took out Johnny and put Rick back in. "You're not getting off your feet, Johnny," he said, tapping Johnny's right leg with his big hand. "What the matter, big guy? No spring in those long legs?"

"Guess not," replied Johnny lamely.

"Exercise them," advised the coach. "Walk and run all you can. And jump. You'll notice the difference."

Johnny nodded.

The Astro Jets led 26 to 19 when the half ended. Both teams went downstairs to their locker rooms for a rest. When they returned Johnny caught a glimpse of two familiar fig-ures walking toward the stands at the far end of the court. Mom and Dad!

He sat on the bench as the second half started and hoped he would stay there the rest of the game. But near the end of the third quarter Coach Dates sent him back in to replace Rick.

He tried to do better, to avoid traveling, to avoid making a foul, to outjump an opponent at the boards or when a jump ball was called. It seemed that the harder he tried the worse he played.

"You outjumped him again, Stogy!" a Jet player shouted.

The Jets scored on the play. A few seconds later Cotton flipped a pass to Johnny near the basket and Johnny sank it. The crowd cheered. But the cheer didn't sound sincere. It seemed to mock him, as if Johnny had sunk the basket by accident.

Johnny sat on the bench during most of the fourth quarter. He went in when there was a minute left to play. He didn't score.

The Astro Jets won, 68 to 57. Johnny couldn't get showered and out of the locker room fast enough.

"Those fans," said Mom irritably as they rode home in Dad's car. "The nerve yelling such awful things. I don't want you to go to another game, Johnny. I don't want you to play again. It's embarrassing."

"Now wait a minute, Celia," said Dad. "Don't ask Johnny to quit. That will only make things worse for him. Fans are like that. Whether they see kids play, or grownups, they like to pick on someone. It's part of the game. Johnny's a good target. He's tall. He has long legs. The fans think he should jump higher than anyone else out there."

"It's ridiculous," muttered Mom.

"Well, there is some truth to that," said Dad, and turned to look back at his stepson for a moment. "You really don't have spring in your legs, Johnny. But practice should take care of that."

"Coach Dates told me to walk and run and jump all I can," said Johnny.

"That'll do it," Dad said with a smile.

4

Bundled in coats, hats, and boots, Johnny and Toby bucked the stiff wind and heavy flakes of snow as they headed for the Community Hall gym and the game against the Hornets.

The hall lay in the direction of the long hill where the boys had gone tobogganing. It was about a third of a mile from home. Dad would have driven them but it was only four-thirty and he was still at work. Johnny didn't mind walking, though. Since Coach had suggested that he exercise his legs and jump as often as possible, he preferred to walk.

Rick Davis started at center against the Hornets. Jim Sain, tall and trim in his green uniform, was in the Hornets left forward position.

The referee tossed the ball up between the centers, blew the whistle, and the game was on. Rick outjumped the Hornets center and tapped the ball to Toby. Toby flipped it to Huck and Huck dribbled it toward the White Cats basket. He stopped as Jim sprang in front of him, pivoted on his left foot, and whipped a pass to Rick. Rick broke for the basket, went up for a layup, and missed. He and Jim Sain leaped for the rebound and Jim got it.

Jim dribbled the ball upcourt, slowed down as he crossed the center line, then suddenly drove in and laid it up against the boards. A basket.

"That-a-way, Jim!" a deep voice thundered from the stands. "Buzz, boy! Buzz!"

Johnny saw the fan on the top seat at the opposite side of the court, a man wearing a shabby gray topcoat and holding a battered old hat.

Seconds later the Hornets scored another basket. Then Rick sank a twenty-foot set shot and Toby followed up with a corner shot that tied the score.

Soon Jim laid up another and the fan wearing the shabby coat yelled, "You're buzzing like a real hornet, Jim, boy!"

Half a minute later Jim tried to lay one up again and Stitch fouled him. Jim took two shots and missed them both. There was a wild scramble under the basket and Jim came up with the ball. He drove in and sank it for his sixth point of the game.

"Okay, Johnny," said Coach Dates. "Take Huck's place."

As Johnny went in Huck said to him, "Good luck." Jim Sain was his man.

Johnny and Jim shook hands. "About time," said Jim. "I've been anxious to see you in action."

White Cats' ball out. Toby tossed it in to Rick. Johnny ran down center court, keeping several paces ahead of Jim. He lifted his hand now and then, trying to catch Rick's attention. Suddenly Rick heaved the ball and Johnny caught it. An instant later another pair of hands grabbed it and the ball was going nowhere.

Shreeeek! "Jump!" yelled the ref.

Johnny and Jim faced each other, their knees bent slightly in readiness to spring. Up went the ball. The boys jumped. Johnny saw Jim's hand go almost a foot above his. Jim tapped the ball and a Hornet grabbed it and dribbled away.

The quarter ended with the Hornets leading 11 to 8.

"Got to get spring in those legs of yours,

Johnny," said Coach Dates as the White Cats grouped around him. "You should be able to jump higher than anybody on the floor."

Johnny avoided his eyes. He accepted the towel handed him and wiped the sweat from his face and arms. Someone was always reminding him of his long legs and poor jumping. Think he didn't know? Why didn't they leave him alone?

He was determined to guard Jim closer than ever during the second quarter. Jim, with a lot of spring in his legs, was a good rebounder. But he was a slow dribbler.

Hornets' ball. A Hornet threw it in from out of bounds and a few passes later Jim had it dribbling upcourt. Johnny saw his chance and rushed in.

He stole the ball from Jim and whipped it to Cotton. A roar broke from the Cats fans. "Nice steal, Johnny!"

Cotton brought the ball back downcourt and passed to Toby. Toby stopped near the corner, aimed for the basket, and shot. In!

Johnny got another chance to steal the ball from Jim. This time Jim grabbed it though, and both boys fought for its possession before the referee's whistle stopped them.

"Jump!"

Johnny dreaded the moment. *Here we go again,* he thought.

Up went the ball. And up leaped Jim and himself. And Jim outjumped him.

A few minutes later the half ended with the Hornets leading, 28 to 25.

Johnny didn't start the second half. He didn't go in until the third quarter was nearly half over. Jim Sain was out so Johnny's man was new to him.

It wasn't long, however, before Jim was in the game again. His presence made a big difference, Johnny saw. Jim was the Hornets' best player. No doubt about it.

In the fourth quarter Johnny tried to stop Jim from sinking a layup and fouled him. The ball had gone in so Jim was given one shot. He sank it and cast a sly grin at Johnny. "Thanks, Johnny," he said. "You can foul me anytime you want to."

Later Johnny took a pass from Cotton, feinted by Jim, and sank a hook shot. It was a nice play and the crowd gave him a big hand. Jim took the throw-in from out of bounds, dribbled to the center line, then bounced a pass under Johnny's right arm to a Hornet teammate. Johnny watched Jim closely, expecting a throw back to him. Jim dashed for the basket and reached for a pass. Johnny stretched out his hand, intercepted the ball, and passed to Huck. He paid little attention to the cheer that went up for him.

He glanced at the clock. Fifty seconds to go. The Hornets were leading 61 to 49. Toby sank a corner shot to make it 61 to 51. Then Jim took another rebound away from Johnny and laid the ball up for two points just as the whistle shrilled, ending the game.

Jim grinned cockily at Johnny. "Told you I'd get even with you tonight," he said, as they headed for the locker room.

"There will be another time," replied Johnny.

It was snowing hard when he and Toby left the Community Hall and headed for home. Suddenly he felt a sharp blow against his back. He started to turn and ducked. A snowball whizzed past his head. Jim Sain and a couple of other Hornets were pegging snowballs.

"Let's run," said Toby.

Johnny quickly took the lead. He turned sharply off the sidewalk, ran up the high snow piled along the side of the street and down the other side toward the street when he saw a monstrous, light-blinking object advancing less than a dozen yards away. A snowplow!

Panic seized Johnny. He slipped and slid down the bank of snow. At the same time he saw the right wing of the huge blade bearing toward him, shooting up a white spray of snow. He heard a scream as the blade struck him. And then his name, "Johnny!"

5

A hand touched his face and he heard a man's deep anxious voice. "Hey, boy. Look at me."

Johnny opened his eyes and blinked against the falling snow. A broad grin spread across a wrinkled face against which the strong headlight of the snowplow was shining.

"That-a-boy," said the man. "You hurt any place, son?"

Johnny tried to think where he might be hurt. "My side a little. And my right leg," he said weakly.

"Just lie still," advised the man. "We'll get an ambulance, take you to a hospital." He looked at his companion, a man in a heavy parka beside him. "Stay with him, Ken. I'll phone for an ambulance."

Presently there was Toby's face above him, eyes peering worriedly. "You hurt bad, Johnny? Something broken?"

"I don't think so, Toby." He moved his hips, his arms, his legs.

"Better lie still, kid," suggested the man named Ken. "A doctor can tell better than you."

Johnny looked pleadingly at Toby. He didn't want to be taken to a hospital. He didn't want Mom and Dad to be worried about him. Especially Mom. She was always deathly afraid of his getting hurt. What was she going to do now? Force him to quit basketball? Would Dad feel the same way?

Other faces appeared in a ring above him.

37

One was Jim Sain's. His eyes were wide, anxious.

Presently the first man returned and said that an ambulance was on its way. Ten minutes later it arrived. Johnny was laid into a stretcher, put into the ambulance, and driven away. Toby was allowed to go with him.

"It was Jim Sain's fault," said Toby angrily.

"I should have seen the snowplow," said Johnny. "But I didn't."

A doctor examined him in the emergency room of the hospital. Mom and Dad had been summoned and were there in five minutes. Their faces were pale and tense with worry.

"What happened, Johnny?" Mom asked in a thin, strained voice. "Tell me what happened. Toby, did you see the accident?"

"He ran across the road and didn't see the snowplow in time," explained Toby. "It was snowing awfully hard."

The doctor tapped Johnny on the legs after a while and smiled. "He'll be all right. Nothing's broken. His heavy coat must have cushioned him from the blow. Take him home and put him to bed. He'll be all right in the morning."

Johnny felt fine the next morning but Mom asked him to stay home from school anyway. He expected her to say that he had to quit basketball but she didn't.

He got fidgety hanging around the house all morning. Mom must have noticed it, for she let him go to school in the afternoon.

He saw Jim look at him in surprise, but Jim said nothing and neither did he. Other guys wanted to know how he was. "Okay," he said simply.

Okay or not, Mom and Dad didn't permit him to play against the Red Foxes on Thursday. Since the game was at six-thirty, however, they all went to see it.

Johnny heard a familiar voice shouting during the game and saw the man in the shabby coat and battered hat. *What an oddball*, thought Johnny. *This time the guy was rooting for the Red Foxes. Probably because the Foxes were the underdog,* Johnny assumed. *But what was he doing here now? Wasn't he a Hornet fan?*

Later Johnny heard another familiar voice. He looked around and saw Jim Sain sitting with other Hornet players on the top row, and suddenly he knew why the man in the bedraggled clothes was here. The Hornets had played the five o'clock game that afternoon and most of the players, and the man, were staying to watch the White Cats–Red Foxes game.

Toby played his usual cool game and scored nine points. Rick led with thirteen. The White Cats took the win, 57 to 49.

Johnny started to leave the floor when a

voice at his side said quietly, "Sorry about the other night, Johnny."

Johnny spun and looked directly into Jim Sain's eyes. *Did I hear right?* he thought. *Did he say he was sorry?*

"That's okay," murmured Johnny, too stunned to say any more.

The White Cats tangled with the Leopards on the 21st and Johnny had his first opportunity to play against the Dunk, Oscar Hill. The Leopards wore black uniforms with white trim and the face of a leopard was painted on the front of their jerseys.

They started off hot as fire. The Dunk sank three baskets to put them in the lead, 6 to 0.

Johnny laid one up and then Toby sank one from his favorite spot, the corner. A jump ball was called when Johnny and Oscar came down with the ball from the boards. Once again Johnny, a few inches taller than the Dunk, failed to outjump his opponent.

The Cats went into the lead in the second quarter. In the third Johnny struck the Dunk's hands twice as the boy went up for layups. Both times the Dunk scored baskets.

In the fourth Johnny struck the Dunk accidentally across the face as they both went up for a rebound. *Shreek!* went the whistle and the ref pointed the penalty finger at Johnny.

"One shot!" he said.

"What?" yelled Johnny and instant anger swelled inside of him. Without thinking he heaved the ball hard against the floor and watched it bounce halfway up to the ceiling. *Shreeek!* went the whistle again.

"Technical!" shouted the ref and glared at Johnny. "One more exhibition like that and you're out of the game, sonny," he warned.

6

The Dunk took two shots — one for the foul Johnny had committed on him, the other for the technical — and sank them both.

Toby took out the ball for the White Cats and passed to Cotton. Cotton bounced it to Stitch and Stitch passed to Johnny, who started to run down the far side of the court.

Johnny saw the Dunk sprinting hard in an effort to intercept the ball and stretched his arms out for it just an instant before the Dunk got there. The Dunk then guarded him like a hawk, crowding him, and Johnny tried to pivot out of his way.

The whistle shrilled and Johnny stared at the ref. *What did I do now?* he wanted to yell.

The ref spun his hands. Traveling! Johnny took the ball in one hand and was about to strike it against the floor again but caught himself in time. He swung the ball around in a swift, graceful arc and tossed it gently to the man in the striped shirt.

He glanced at the scoreboard. The White Cats were leading by two points, 57 to 55. What a surprise! He had thought sure that the Leopards were ahead.

A Leopard sank a long one. At the whistle a horn buzzed and Johnny saw Nat Newton coming into the game. Nat pointed at him and Johnny trotted off the court. He didn't go in again. The game went to the White Cats, 63 to 59.

"You've got to learn to control your temper, Johnny," Coach Dates warned in the locker room. "Bouncing the ball like you did is bad medicine."

Johnny forced a grin. "I caught myself just in time when he called that traveling violation on me," he said. "He sure would've thrown me out of the game then."

"You're darn right he would have," said the coach. "If he didn't, I would have."

"You did, anyway," Johnny chuckled.

In the car Mom made the remark again that Johnny ought to give up basketball. "Everyone picks on him," she said. "No one is even giving him a chance to get adjusted."

"I can't quit, Ma," said Johnny. "I told you that. You just can't quit because of things like that."

"Johnny's right, Celia," said Dad. "Quitting isn't the way out of it. Johnny likes basketball. He'll get used to the rules gradually.

He'll get to be quite a jumper, too. He'll get some knocks and bruises on the way but that's part of the game. Right, Johnny?"

"It sure is," said Johnny.

Mom argued the point a little further, then gave up. She probably realized that this was one situation that whatever she said would not change their minds.

Dad and the boys had cleared the snow away from the front of the garage, so Johnny took every available opportunity to practice jumping. Toby got Dad's step-ladder and drew a chalk mark on the backboard where Johnny's fingertips touched.

"The day I'd like to see is when you out-jump Jim Sain," said Toby. "If anybody gives me a pain it's him."

The Swordtails played the White Cats on Thursday and took the game 61 to 50. Johnny scored eleven points. He was sure he would have scored more had he been able to outjump the Swordtails' lanky center, Steve Kadish.

Friday afternoon was Christmas Eve. Dad took it off and he, Grandpa, and the boys went after a Christmas tree. They cut one down at a local farm, placed it on a stand in the living room, and decorated it that night. Christmas packages were piled underneath it and opened the next morning. Dad shot flash pictures as the boys, Mom, and Grandpa opened their packages.

Johnny choked back tears as he unwrapped a sweater, two shirts, socks, two books on undersea adventure, and a camera set. Toby got clothes too, plus a new stamp album and books on tropical fish.

What a Christmas, thought Johnny. *What a real happy Christmas. It was only Mom and me before. Now there are five of us.*

It was snowing thick flakes but Grandpa, Dad, Mom, and the boys walked the three blocks to church. Afterwards Mom cooked a big dinner — baked ham with pineapple slices, potatoes, corn, pickles, and pie. In the afternoon they went tobogganing. All except Grandpa.

"I was young enough last year," he said. "But this year I'm too old for that sort of stuff."

Mom, Dad, and the boys rode the toboggan together. Mom screamed and laughed most of the way down the hill. Johnny had never seen her so happy. *Even though I'm having my problems with basketball,* he thought, *Mom and I have been the happiest we've ever been since the day she remarried and we came to live with Dad, Grandpa, and Toby.*

Mom and Dad got tired after a few rides and went home. About four o'clock the boys decided to call it quits too. They had walked a short distance on the road toward home when a sleigh, drawn by two horses, started to pass by them.

"Hey, Johnny! Toby!" yelled a familiar voice. It was Stitch Buttons. "Hitch your rope to the back and I'll pull you!"

"Great!" cried Johnny.

He looped the rope around a metal peg on the right side, then sat on the toboggan with Toby. Stitch cracked his reins lightly over the horses and they started off again.

"You never did this in New York City, did you?" cried Toby, laughing.

"I guess not!" said Johnny happily.

They reached the first house in town and Johnny heard some boys shouting to Stitch. Seconds later two boys passed by the sleigh, pulling sleds toward the distant hill.

"Well, look who's getting a ride," one of the boys exclaimed. "Hi, Johnny! Hi, Toby!"

Suddenly there was a loud shout and Johnny saw Jim Sain leaping from behind a bush and yelling at the horses. One of the horses whinnied in fear and reared up on its hind legs.

"Hey, cut that out!" shouted Stitch.

But the sleigh started speeding down the street. Johnny and Toby grabbed the side rails of the toboggan to keep from being jolted off.

"Halt!" yelled Stitch. "Halt!"

The horses seemed to run even faster.

People on the sidewalks began to scream. *What if we knock someone down?* thought Johnny, panic-stricken. *What if we hit a car?*

The horses swung to the right at the corner. The sleigh started to swing, too. Its rear end skidded toward the left side of the street, missing a car by inches. Just then the toboggan rolled over, spilling Johnny and Toby out onto the street.

7

The boys rolled over and over until they hit a snowbank. They sat up and stared dazedly at each other. "You okay?" asked Johnny shakily.

"Yes. Are you?"

"I think so."

They looked down the street at the sleigh and at Stitch pulling hard on the reins in a desperate effort to stop the horses. Near the end of the block the horses slowed down and came to an abrupt halt, lifting their front hoofs high into the air and whinnying loudly.

"Stitch has stopped them," observed Johnny. "Come on."

They ran down the street. Stitch was looking back at them. "You guys okay?" he shouted.

"Yes!" cried Johnny. He reached the sleigh and unhooked the rope of the toboggan.

"That darn Jim Sain," Stitch said angrily. "He did it. He scared the horses."

Stitch looked down the street behind him. Johnny looked too and saw Jim come running around the corner with the other boys at his heels. They stopped instantly and Stitch shouted, "I'm going to tell the police about this, Sain! They'll fix you!"

Jim turned, walked back up the street, and vanished around the corner, his friends with him.

A policeman came running from the opposite direction.

"What's the trouble, young fella?" he

asked Stitch. "Those horses get away from you?"

"A kid jumped from behind a bush and scared them," said Stitch. "They started running and I couldn't stop them for a while. They're okay now."

"Good. Move on. You're holding up traffic."

Johnny wondered if Stitch was going to tell the policeman who the kid was, but Stitch didn't. He slapped the reins and the horses moved on.

Johnny and Toby walked up on the sidewalk, pulling the toboggan after them. "Jim Sain's a real pain," grumbled Toby. "He's always doing something to make people mad. Why can't he do something good for a change?"

"Maybe he's unhappy," said Johnny.

"Unhappy? Why should he be unhappy?"

Johnny shrugged. "I don't know. But look

at the clothes he wears to school. They're hardly ever clean and he wears the same pair of jeans over and over. And he hasn't had a haircut since I've been here. Maybe he doesn't have anything and gets his kicks by being dirty to people."

"Guess we're lucky," reflected Toby. "Especially since you and Mom came to live with us."

Johnny smiled and put an arm over Toby's shoulders. "You know what? I didn't know what to think at first. I was scared having a new brother, a father, and a grandfather all of a sudden. I didn't think I could have fun in a small town, either."

Toby's eyes flashed warmth. "Are you glad now you came?"

"Darn right. I wouldn't change this for a million bucks."

8

School was closed till Monday, January 3. Johnny had lots of time to practice jumping and jump shots. Especially jumping, because he needed that most of all. He practiced several times a day and noticed that he was already jumping higher than before.

"You're gaining," said Toby, drawing a new chalk mark where Johnny's fingertips touched the backboard. "About two inches."

Two inches, thought Johnny. *He had a lot to go to outjump Jim Sain and Oscar Hill*.

The White Cats played the Astro Jets in the school gym on Tuesday, December 28.

Johnny laid in a basket within the first thirty seconds. He still had trouble with his pivot foot. He couldn't pivot without dragging it across the floor a few inches, drawing a whistle from the referee for a traveling violation.

He remembered not to lose his temper though. He wouldn't forget the ref's warning when he had deliberately bounced the ball hard against the floor.

He was still unable to grab a rebound from the Astro Jets' tall center. He was hearing a name more often too. A name someone had tacked onto him several games back.

"Come on, Johnny Long Legs! Jump!"

He and Stogy Giles caught a rebound at the same time when the score was 7 to 4 in the White Cats' favor. The referee tossed the ball up between them and Johnny tried to put all the spring he could into his legs to outjump the boy who was more than six inches shorter than he. Stogy still outjumped him.

Other than Stogy, however, the Jets had no one with a sharp eye for the basket. One of them tried a shot from the center line and made it. The fans for both teams cheered for him. But apparently his shot was just lucky. It was the only one he made that first half.

The White Cats went into the second half leading 31 to 18. Stogy had made twelve of the eighteen points. He was small but fast. Twice he had stolen the ball from Johnny, leaving Johnny stunned for a second. And embarrassed.

Nat Newton played the last two minutes of the third quarter in place of Johnny and also started the fourth quarter. Johnny didn't mind. He hoped Coach Dates would keep him on the bench the rest of the game.

He was tired of people calling him Johnny Long Legs and making fun of his poor jumping.

There were four minutes left in the quarter when the coach sent him back in. "Two things to remember, Johnny," he said. "Watch your pivot foot, and put all the spring into your legs that you can when you jump." Then he added, "You don't like the fans calling you Johnny Long Legs, do you? Ignore them. Know what fans used to call me when I played ball? Mucilage. It means glue. What do you think of *that* name?"

Johnny laughed. He agreed that it was certainly worse than Johnny Long Legs.

He fouled Stogy when the little guy tried to dribble by him and Stogy was given a shot. He made it. Then Johnny scored a set. A few seconds later he intercepted a pass, dribbled fast upcourt, and laid the ball against the boards for another two points.

The game ended with the White Cats winning, 64 to 49.

"Good game, Johnny," said Toby as they headed for the locker room. "You were high scorer."

"How many?" asked Johnny.

"Twenty-seven points. Not bad, huh?"

They took their showers and began dressing when Nat Newton said something that was news to Johnny. "Did you hear that Coach Smith kicked Jim Sain off the Hornets because of what he had done to Stitch Buttons' horses?"

Johnny stared at him. "Are you sure?"

"Sure, I'm sure."

"He deserves it," said Rick. "Jim's always horsing around. Wising it up. It's about time somebody did something with him."

"I don't know," said Johnny thoughtfully as he and Toby walked home after the game. "Do you think the coach should have kicked

Jim off the team just because he yelled and scared the horses?"

Toby shrugged. "Don't you?"

"No. Maybe benching him for a while would be okay. But kicking him off the team . . . Man!"

"Yeah," said Toby. "That is pretty rough."

"And did you see that look on his face? He looked scared. Real scared."

"He sure did," admitted Toby.

They walked the rest of the way home in silence.

Toby told Mom and Dad about Coach Smith's tossing Jim Sain off the Hornets for what Jim had done, and also told them how Johnny felt about it. Dad smiled at Johnny. "This interests me, son. After the trouble Jim Sain has caused you and Toby, you think that his coach is giving him a raw deal. Both of you could've been badly hurt if it weren't for that snowbank, you know."

"I know," said Johnny. Then he looked at Mom. *You understand, don't you, Mom? You've seen kids like Jim Sain in New York City. They do things to hurt you, then are sorry afterwards.*

Mom put an arm around his shoulders and gave him a hug. "I think I know why Johnny feels the way he does about Jim," she said. "We both have seen boys like Jim in New York. I don't know this boy Jim. But if Johnny wants to help him I don't see anything wrong in that. Do you?" she asked her husband.

"Not at all. Tell you what, son. Why don't you telephone Mr. Smith and ask him to give Jim another chance? He just might do it."

Johnny thought about the suggestion. *It's not that easy,* he wanted to say.

"Can I wait till tomorrow?" he asked.

"Sure," said Dad, patting him on the shoulder. "Take time to think about it."

Johnny thought about it most of the next day. That evening he gathered all the courage he could and telephoned Mr. Smith.

"Mr. Smith," he began, "this is Johnny Reese. My brother and I were on the toboggan that spilled over after Jim Sain had . . ." He wet his lips. His heart was pounding. ". . . after he had scared those horses."

"Yes. I know who you are," said Mr. Smith. "What do you want, Johnny?"

"Well, I heard you took Jim off the team because of what he'd done. I just thought — well, when we lived in New York City I knew a lot of guys. Some of them were like Jim Sain. They did mean things but, really, the guys weren't bad. I mean they were unhappy because their mothers and fathers never looked after them. I hardly know Jim, but the way he comes to school and the way he acts . . . I don't know, Mr. Smith. I think

62

he's just unhappy and does things to . . . well . . . It's hard to explain, Mr. Smith."

"I think I know what you mean, Johnny," said Mr. Smith.

"Well, the reason I called is to ask if you'd give him another chance." A lump rose in Johnny's throat.

"I see," said Mr. Smith. "Okay, Johnny. I appreciate your telling me this. I'll think about it and decide what to do. Okay?"

"Okay. Thanks, Mr. Smith."

"You're very welcome, Johnny."

Johnny hung up. Sweat was rolling down his face.

The White Cats played the Hornets in the Community Hall on Thursday. Johnny looked anxiously for Jim Sain as the Hornets trotted in from the locker room. There he was!

"He's playing," Toby said beside him.

"Talking to Coach Smith did it, Johnny. I hope he knows it was you who helped put him back on the team."

Johnny didn't get in the game until the first quarter was half over. As before Coach Dates played him opposite Jim Sain. Jim was the first to put out his hand as Johnny came across the floor.

"Johnny, thanks for talking to the coach," he said.

Johnny smiled. "Forget it."

Toby tossed the ball to Rick from out of bounds. Rick dribbled it a few steps and passed to Stitch. Stitch's guard almost took the ball from him. He stumbled backwards and rolled the ball across the floor to Johnny. Both Johnny and Jim Sain raced after it. They got it at the same time and struggled for its possession.

Shreeek! "Jump!" yelled the ref.

Johnny and Jim faced each other. The ref stood before them.

From the stands came a fan's yell. The voice of the man Johnny had heard too often already. "Don't let Leadfoot outjump you, Jim!"

Up went the ball. And up went the boys, Johnny leaping as high as he could. But it wasn't high enough. Jim's fingers soared a couple of inches higher. It was close. Closer than ever before.

9

A Hornet dribbled the ball cautiously across the center line then passed it to a teammate in the left corner. The player tried to take a shot but Toby leaped in front of him and forced him to toss the ball to another teammate.

The ball passed from one Hornet to another. Then Jim had it, took a shot, and scored.

Johnny shook his head disgustedly, turned, and ran upcourt. He had to keep Jim Sain from making baskets. At least keep him from making as many as he was accustomed to. It would be something if Jim was a star today and won the game for the Hornets. *I'd be the goat*, thought Johnny, *for I'm the one who pleaded with Coach Smith to let Jim play*.

The game was tied at the end of the first quarter, 11 to 11. In the second quarter the Hornets broke the tie when a little red-headed boy sank a corner shot. The ball struck the net without touching the rim.

The White Cats tossed the ball in from out of bounds. Cotton Cornish dribbled it across the center line, then whipped it to Stitch Buttons. A fiery Hornet went after Stitch and Stitch passed to Johnny.

Johnny considered taking a shot. He was just outside of the foul-shooting lane and not far from the basket. But in a wink Jim was there in front of him, his arms beating up and down like the wings of a humming-bird. Johnny passed to Rick.

Rick dribbled toward the basket, went up, and shot. At the same time a Hornet struck his wrist. *Shreeeek!* went the whistle. The ball swiveled through the net.

The ref signaled that the basket counted and that Rick was entitled to one shot. Rick made it, putting the Cats ahead, 14 to 13.

The Hornets took the ball down to their basket, tried to move in close with it, but couldn't. The Cats had formed a human wall to defend the basket. Only a daring player would try to break through it.

A daring player did. Jim Sain. He broke through the wall, with his right shoulder striking Cotton so hard that Cotton fell. The whistle shrilled as Jim leaped under the basket, laid the ball up against the boards, and sank it.

The ref shook his head sideways and yelled, "No basket!" Then he pointed a finger at Jim. "Charging!" he said, and gave the ball to the White Cats.

Jim made a face then ran downcourt to help defend his basket. Johnny and Toby exchanged grins. That time Jim's daring charge had backfired.

Toby took out the ball and passed it to Johnny. Johnny tossed it to Cotton, who he figured was a better dribbler than himself. Cotton dribbled to the center line where a Hornet buzzed at him and made a stab for the ball. Cotton stopped on a dime, pivoted on his right foot, and passed to Rick. Rick faked a shot and then passed to Toby, who was running down the right sideline. Toby caught the ball, stopped to shoot, but two players swarmed upon him instantly. One clamped his hand on the ball, trapping it.

Jump ball.

Toby outjumped his opponent but a Hornet caught the tap and started upcourt in a fast sprint. There was no White Cat within yards of him. He leaped, laid the ball nicely against the boards, and scored two points.

Again Toby took out the ball. He wasn't grinning now. Neither was Johnny. Johnny caught the pass from Toby and bounced it to Rick. Rick passed to Cotton, who again dribbled the ball to the center line, then across it, where a Hornet stopped him.

Cotton passed to Nat Newton who was in for Stitch. Nat dribbled to the left sideline then passed to Huck, who was running in toward the basket. Huck caught the pass and laid it up. Two points.

The game moved along swiftly, both teams playing equally well. The score remained close with the lead changing from one team to the other and back again.

At the midway point of the second quarter Coach Dates put in Ken Addison in place of

Rick and Dale Michaels in place of Toby. A couple of minutes later he sent in Buzz Elliot in place of Cotton. Johnny noticed that Coach Smith had put in substitutes too.

The fresh new players made little difference with the score. It was a tie seconds before the half ended. Ken sank one from the corner to break it, putting the Cats in the lead, 31 to 29, when the whistle blew.

Johnny was glad for the intermission. He was tired and the rest would do him good. He had played the entire first half.

He started the second half too. Hardly half a minute passed when Jim had the ball, dribbling toward the Cats basket. Johnny sprang after him. *I'm going to stop this shot,* he promised himself, *even if I foul him.*

He brushed past a Hornet and put his hand flat against the ball as Jim started to leap. Jim scarcely got off the floor. He looked from the basket to the player who had stopped him and Johnny thought he had never seen a more surprised look on anybody's face than was on Jim's.

"Jump!" yelled the ref.

The two boys faced each other. The ref stood ready to toss the ball up between them.

"Outjump him, Jim!" yelled that familiar voice again.

Johnny waited anxiously for the ref to toss up the ball. He was determined to jump higher than Jim this time.

The ball went up. The boys jumped. Johnny saw Jim's hand rise up past his, saw the hand tap the ball to a Hornet teammate.

"That-a-boy, Jim!" yelled the fan.

The Hornet tried a long shot. This time Johnny caught the ball as it bounced off the boards. He tossed it to Dale. Dale dribbled it a few steps then passed to Buzz. Buzz passed to Ken, who dribbled down the right sideline and took a set from the corner. A basket!

Johnny glanced at the scoreboard. The Cats were ahead by four points, 33 to 29.

The game remained close to the very end. The Cats led 54 to 53 with ten seconds left to play. The ball was in their possession.

"Hold that ball!" shouted Coach Dates. "Don't lose it!"

Johnny had the ball. He started to pass it to Rick but Jim got to it and tried to yank it away. Jump ball.

Now, thought Johnny. *I've got to outjump him now.*

He didn't. Jim tapped the ball to a teammate. Seconds later the Hornets scored. Two seconds later the horn blew. The game was over. 55 to 54, Hornets.

The Hornet fans roared their heads off. Both teams shook hands with each other. "Nice game, Jim," said Johnny.

Just then a man with a broad, happy smile on his face came forward and put an arm around Jim's shoulders. It was the man in the shabby coat. The man who called Johnny "Leadfoot" and "Long Legs."

"Beautiful game, Jim," he said proudly. "You played like a champ."

"Thanks, Pop," said Jim.

10

Johnny stared. Then he turned and headed for the locker room.

So the man was Jim's father. He should have guessed.

"Hey, Johnny! Wait!"

Johnny looked behind him. Jim came running toward him. "My pop said that he's not going home right away. Want to come over?"

Again Johnny could hardly believe his ears. *What a change,* he thought. *He made me spill my milk, threw snowballs at me, scared a team of horses so that Toby and I were nearly badly hurt. Now he's inviting me to his home.*

"Okay," he agreed. Suddenly a thought occurred to him. Since Jim's pop wasn't going home anyway, why not invite Jim to his house?

Johnny posed the question, adding that Jim could eat there, too. He felt sure that Mom would cook enough food for an extra mouth.

Jim's face colored slightly. "Oh. I don't know."

He wants to come, thought Johnny. *But he's ashamed to.*

"Come on," Johnny insisted. "I'll have you meet my folks."

"You sure it's okay? About eating there, I mean?"

"Sure, I'm sure. Unless you eat like a horse!" laughed Johnny.

They walked to the locker room together. After they showered and dressed Jim asked Johnny for the use of his comb. Johnny let him. *Doesn't he even own a comb?*

Toby, Johnny, and Jim walked home together. "You can telephone your mother from our house," suggested Johnny. "She might wonder what happened to you."

"I don't have a mother," said Jim.

Toby and Johnny looked at him.

"She died a while back," Jim explained quietly. "There's only my pop and me."

"Where are your grandparents?"

"They don't live around here." Jim paused, scooped up a handful of snow, formed a ball out of it, and pegged it against a light pole. Smack! It struck the pole and scattered in all directions, leaving a big white eye.

They arrived home and Johnny introduced Jim to Mom and Dad. "Okay if Jim eats supper with us, Mom? You made enough, didn't you?"

She smiled. "I made plenty," she said. "Do you like fried chicken and rice, Jim?"

"Oh, sure. I eat anything."

Johnny saw how hungrily Jim tackled his meal, as if he hadn't eaten in days.

After dinner Toby showed Jim his new stamp album. He started to explain the history of each stamp he had placed in the album — both United States and foreign — and got so enthusiastic about it that Johnny thought for sure that Toby would spend half the night at it unless he was stopped.

"Okay, okay, Toby," he said. "What do you want to do, turn Jim into a stamp collector?"

"I was just explaining . . ." began Toby.

"Sure you were. But maybe Jim isn't as nuts about stamps as you are."

Jim grinned. "That's okay. Don't you guys go fighting about it."

"Let's show him our aquarium," suggested Johnny.

The brothers showed Jim their aquarium. It was a twenty-gallon tank, explained Toby, who took the job of describing it and the fish in it as if they belonged only to him. Johnny stood back silently, feeling somewhat out of the picture. The aquarium was here before he had come. Even though Dad had said that it was his as much as Toby's, Toby still seemed to think it was only his.

"See that pair there?" Toby pointed at two silver-spangled fish with long blue dorsal and gold pectoral fins. "They're called severums. And those pretty purple ones are guppies."

"What do they eat?" asked Jim.

"Fish food," said Toby.

"Frozen shrimp," explained Johnny specifically. "We keep it in the refrigerator. There's also fish food in those boxes under the aquarium."

Jim watched the fish swimming around inside the tank for a long time. Now and then a fish chased its mate, then stopped and nibbled at a green plant growing from the base of tiny blue and red stones. Johnny, too, enjoyed watching them. The beautiful angel fish with their long fins, the black-striped tiger barbs, the homely whiskered catfish lying quietly on the bottom. They swam slowly, then darted swiftly; they romped like children.

"They're really pretty," said Jim finally. "I've never seen tropical fish before."

At eight o'clock Jim said he'd better go home. His pop was probably home by now, waiting for him.

"May I go with him, Ma?" asked Johnny.

"Okay. But don't stay long. It's getting late."

Jim's house was on a country road, a ten-minute walk from Johnny's house. The wind was blowing hard, singing around Johnny's ears and whipping snow against his face. He remembered the night he had fallen in front of the moving snowplow because of Jim's throwing snowballs at him. Now suddenly they were friends.

Mr. Sain wasn't home. "He'll be home soon," said Jim. "He's probably visiting some friend of his."

"Want me to stay awhile?" asked Johnny. "Till your father comes home?"

Jim shrugged. "Sure."

They took off their boots in the kitchen, hung up their coats and hats, then sat at the kitchen table. The room was large, the stove was an old range, the wallpaper old and drab.

"Just a second," said Jim. He hurried out of the room and Johnny heard him climbing stairs. There was an ashtray on the middle of the table, partly smoked cigarettes in it. Johnny remembered the butt he had picked up when he and Toby had gone tobogganing. He went to his coat and unzipped the pocket. There was the butt. He took it out just as Jim returned, carrying several large sheets of paper.

"I did these," he said, placing the pile in front of Johnny.

They were pencil drawings of ships — passenger ships, clippers, and sailboats. There were also drawings of the sea — the high waves, the rockbound coast with the waves lashing furiously against it, lighthouses, and men harpooning a whale.

"Hey, they're terrif," exclaimed Johnny. "Did you really do these?"

Jim nodded proudly. "I like anything to do

with the sea. I'd like to be a sailor when I get older."

He saw the butt in Johnny's hand and his eyebrows arched. "Hey, do you smoke?" he asked curiously.

"Used to. Do you?"

"No. Those butts are my father's. Go ahead. Smoke if you want to. I won't squeal."

Johnny thought about it a minute. "Used to," he had said. He remembered the time. There were he and two other boys. The other boys had cigarettes and had dared him to smoke. And he did, just to win the dare. He had almost gagged from the smoke and the taste. He had smoked a couple of times after that but only in the presence of the two boys.

They had thought it was smart. Grown-up. If Mom had known he had smoked she would have skinned him alive. There was

Dad to think about now, too. Neither one would want him to smoke.

"No," he said. "I don't know why I even picked it up. I thought I would put it in here."

He reached over and squashed the butt into the ashtray. Squashed it so that the paper got all torn and the tobacco fell out of it.

11

"How come you asked Coach Smith to let me play again?" asked Jim. "After what I did to you and Toby."

"Forget it," said Johnny.

"I can't forget it. How come?"

Johnny took a deep breath and let it out slowly. "Well, I remembered how you looked at me after I was hit by the snowplow. And how you looked when Toby and I fell off our toboggan."

"How did I look?"

"You looked scared to death."

"I was."

"Anyhow, I knew you were sorry. That's why I called up Coach Smith."

Jim slid back on his chair and stretched his legs out under the table. "I'm sorry I did all those crazy things to you," confessed Jim. "And for making you spill the milk too. Guess it was all kind of stupid."

"Well, let's forget it," said Johnny. "Let's not talk about it anymore."

They were silent awhile. There was no sound except the wind howling like a hungry animal outside.

Finally Johnny broke the silence. "When is your father coming home?"

Jim looked at the clock on the wall. "Anytime now."

He had said that before.

"He really roots for you at the basketball games, doesn't he?" smiled Johnny.

Jim laughed. "Yeah, I know. And I heard

him calling you 'Long Legs' and 'Leadfoot.' Before the game tonight I told him not to call you those names again. He forgot, I guess." He rose from the chair. "Come on. I have some stuff in my room I'll show you."

Jim's bedroom walls were shabby too. Besides the bed there was a chair, a nightstand with a lamp on it, and two orange crates standing on end with books and magazines and a couple of cigar boxes in them.

Jim took two cigar boxes out of a crate, put them on the bed, and opened them. Colored rocks and fossils practically filled each box.

"I like collecting rocks and fossils too," he said proudly.

While looking at the collection Johnny began to smell a strange odor. He lifted a rock to his nose and sniffed at it. There was no smell.

"Hey, look!" Jim exclaimed suddenly.

Johnny looked at the base of the door where Jim was pointing. Smoke!

He dropped the rock into the cigar box and started to run after Jim. Jim flung open the door, but a thick cloud of smoke drove them back into the room. Jim slammed the door shut.

He stared, petrified. "It's our furnace pipes," he said. "Pop kept saying he'd get new ones but he never did."

Johnny paled. "We'd better phone the fire department or this house will burn down to the ground."

"Can't," said Jim. "Our phone was disconnected last week. We can't get out of here, anyway. There's too much smoke coming inside."

Johnny stared at the smoke seeping in underneath the door and curling into the room. The boys covered their eyes against the stinging fog. They coughed and backed against the farthest wall.

"We have to get out of here!" yelled Johnny. "We'll burn to death if we don't!"

"We'll have to jump out of the window!" cried Jim.

"Jump that far? We'll break every bone in our bodies!"

Nevertheless, he went to the window, the only one in the room. It was latched securely on top and at the two lower sides. He unlatched it at the top and tried to lift the window.

It was stuck solid.

12

Jim! Help me!"

Jim grabbed hold of the right side and lifted and Johnny did the same on the left side. The window suddenly broke loose and the boys lifted it as high as it could go.

Cold, refreshing air gushed into the room. The boys inhaled it deeply, let it clean out their lungs. At the same time smoke swirled out in a thick, swirling fog.

Johnny looked out. "The snow looks deep down there, Jim," he said. "We could jump and may not get hurt at all."

"Hurt or not, I'm going to jump, anyway," replied Jim.

Johnny stepped out onto the windowsill, crouched to clear his head from the window above him, and jumped. He sank into the snow. It was deep and he didn't get hurt. Then Jim landed beside him.

"Let's get to a phone," said Johnny, wading through the soft feathery snow toward the sidewalk. He looked over his shoulders at the tongues of flame leaping out of the first-story windows and lapping at the wood frame wall.

"My drawings! My rocks!" screamed Jim, his eyes blurred with tears.

"C'mon!" yelled Johnny. "Let's run to that house and call the fire department!"

"It'll be too late!"

"We still should do it! C'mon!"

They raced to the small house a short distance up the road. The wind snarled around their ears, lashed at their unprotected bodies. Their boots, coats, and hats were in the burning house.

"Jim! Wait!" a voice yelled in the darkness behind them.

They looked back. Mr. Sain was running toward them, his hat gripped in his hand. "Thank the Lord you're okay!"

"We're going over to the Burks' to phone the fire department," said Jim.

"Go ahead. And stay there. I'll stay here and wait for them. And you, Johnny. Better call your parents from there, too. They'll have to come and take you home. You're not going to walk through this cold night like that."

"You won't go into the house for anything, will you, Pop?" inquired Jim worriedly.

"No, son. Don't you worry. It's burning

too hard. There's nothing real important in there, anyway."

Except Jim's drawings, thought Johnny. *And his rocks and fossils.*

They ran to the Burks'. Mr. Burk immediately put in a call to the fire department, then pulled on his boots and winter clothes and dashed out into the night. Johnny telephoned home. He explained to Mom what had happened.

"Dad will come right over," she said in a hurried, nervous voice.

Two fire trucks arrived. They couldn't save the house. The Burks and Jim and Johnny watched through the windows of the Burks' house as the flames devoured it. It was a sad, heartbreaking sight.

Dad had coats and caps for both boys. They met Mr. Sain outside. He was weeping.

"I should've fixed those pipes," he kept saying sadly. "It was my fault."

"Mr. Sain," said Dad, "you and Jim come over and stay with us tonight. We have room."

"No. We can't do that. We'll be imposing."

"Imposing, nothing. Come on. Get into my car. There's no sense standing here any longer."

Mr. Sain got into the car and Jim got in beside him. Johnny sat in front with his father. Mr. Reese started the car and headed for home.

13

Mr. Sain wanted to look for an apartment right after breakfast the next morning. He said he and Jim didn't need a house anymore; a furnished apartment would do. The insurance money that he was going to receive for the burned-down house would be put into the bank for Jim's college education.

Mr. Reese didn't want him and Jim to leave right away though. Not until after the new year. "Stay with us till then," he insisted. "In the meantime, you can look for an apartment."

"Two extra mouths to feed for a few days means nothing," added Mrs. Reese.

Johnny saw the warm look on Jim's face. He knew that Jim wanted his father to accept the invitation.

"Okay," Mr. Sain agreed finally. "We'll stay. Thanks very much. You people have been most kind to Jim and me. Come on, Jim. We'll look for an apartment." He smiled. "See you tonight, Mr. Reese."

"Hollis is my first name," said Mr. Reese. "Call me Hollis."

Mr. Sain put out his hand and Mr. Reese took it. "And mine is Jim, the same as my son's," said Mr. Sain.

During Christmas vacation Johnny did as much jumping as he could. On Sunday, the day before school started again, Toby made a new chalk mark where the tips of Johnny's fingers touched the boards after he had jumped. Then he measured it with a foot ruler.

"Look!" he exclaimed. "A gain of seven inches from the first time!"

Johnny grinned. "I'm getting there," he said.

Jim was there, too. He jumped and Toby made a chalk mark where his fingers had touched. It was exactly two inches below Johnny's.

"I guess you are getting there," exclaimed Jim. "But maybe on a basketball court it'll be different."

"We'll see about that. Won't we, Johnny?" said Toby, his eyes glinting with pride.

Johnny smiled. Toby sure was for him every bit of the way.

On January 4 the White Cats played the Red Foxes. The Cats had beaten the Foxes twice. They had confidence in beating them again. The game was at the school gym.

Since it started at 6:30 Dad could attend. Mom and Grandpa came with him. It was the first game that Grandpa had come to see. Mr. Sain had found an apartment and he and Jim had left that morning.

The Red Foxes' red satin uniforms, the face of a fox painted on the front of the jerseys, looked as if they had just come out of their boxes. They were a colorful contrast to the Cats' white.

Johnny started at the left forward position, playing opposite Butch Hendricks, the Red Foxes' leading scorer. Butch wore glasses and was tall and thin as a reed. At right forward was Huck Stevens. Toby and Cotton played the guard positions and Rick Davis center.

The referee blew his whistle as he tossed the ball up between Rick and Tom Case, the Foxes' center, and the game was on. Tom outjumped Rick and tapped the ball to a teammate. The Fox dribbled it toward the White Cats basket, then stopped as Toby popped in front of him. The Red Fox player tossed the ball to another Fox coming up behind him. The Fox dribbled to the corner, aimed at the basket, and shot. In for two points.

Toby took out the ball and tossed it to Johnny. Johnny dribbled across the center line, bounced the ball to Huck. Huck made a fast break for the basket, stopped inches in front of it, leaped, and shot the ball in a slow arc. In.

Seconds later the ball was again close to the White Cats basket. The Red Foxes tossed it back and forth, waiting for the chance to make a break and shoot. Then, as if he couldn't wait any longer, a Red Fox took a shot. The ball struck the backboard, then the rim, and bounced off.

Johnny and two Red Fox men, including

Tom Case, scrambled for the ball. Johnny and Tom came down with the ball clutched in their hands.

"Jump!" yelled the ref.

The boys faced each other.

The referee tossed up the ball. The boys leaped. Johnny gave his legs all the spring he could. His hands went up beyond Tom's. He tapped the ball!

"That-a-way, Johnny!" a voice cried in the stands. Mr. Sain's voice!

Cotton caught the tap and dribbled down-court. A Red Fox swooped in from behind him, tried to steal the ball. Smack! His hand struck Cotton's. The whistle shrilled.

"One shot!" said the ref.

Cotton took his time at the foul line. He bounced the ball twice, then looked at the basket and shot. The ball arced gracefully and sank in without touching the rim.

The seconds ticked away on the big clock

above the lighted, red-figured scoreboard. When the first four minutes of the first quarter had passed, the score was tied, 7 to 7.

The Red Foxes broke it, scoring a long shot from the center line. The shot was made by Butch Hendricks, Johnny's man.

The Red Foxes widened their lead. Butch scored again and again, each shot from behind the foul line or from a corner. Johnny couldn't stop him.

In the second quarter Butch tried his long shots again. The first one missed. A Red Fox took the ball off the boards and passed it back to Butch. Butch's second try also failed. Again a Red Fox got the rebound. This time he dribbled toward the center line, away from the crowd under the basket. He passed to a teammate going in. The teammate passed to Butch. Like a cat Johnny pounced on the ball at the same time Butch did.

Then both he and Butch had it, each fighting for its possession.

Shreeek! Jump ball.

Again Johnny gave his legs all the spring he possibly could. Up . . . up he went past Butch's hand and tapped the ball to Huck. Huck took it, dribbled toward the center line, and passed to Nat Newton, who had gone in for Toby. Nat dribbled a bit and passed to Johnny running in fast toward the basket. Johnny caught the ball and leaped high. A beautiful layup!

"Nice play, Johnny!" yelled Mr. Sain.

Johnny turned, brushed the sweat off his brow, and ran back upcourt. *Wonder what he'd say if I outjumped Jim,* he thought. *Would he still call me Johnny Long Legs?*

14

The half ended with the Red Foxes leading, 31 to 24.

"Do more shooting this second half, Johnny," said Coach Dates, standing with one foot on a bench in the locker room. "Try more layups." He grinned. "You've come a long way with your jumping. And you've improved your pivoting, too. Goes to show what steady practice will do. And determination."

Johnny sat with his elbows on his knees. Practice? Determination? No one except he and Toby knew how hard he had practiced to improve his jumping and to pivot without dragging his foot across the floor.

The boys went upstairs to start the second half and Johnny did as the coach had advised. Whenever he saw his chance he drove in for a layup. Sometimes he didn't make it, but most of the time he did. Cotton and Huck fed him the ball and sank a few baskets themselves.

By the end of the third quarter they were trailing 49 to 48. The Red Foxes widened their lead by four points but gradually the White Cats gained ground again. With a minute to go in the last quarter the Cats were leading by a very thin margin, 61 to 60.

Then Johnny fouled Butch, striking Butch's hand as he jumped for a layup.

"Two shots!" yelled the ref.

Butch made them both. 62–61, Red Foxes' favor.

Then, with fifteen seconds left, Johnny

got the ball and dribbled it to the corner. Fourteen seconds . . . thirteen . . . twelve . . . Johnny kept dribbling. Butch guarded him like a hawk, trying desperately to keep him from making a fast break.

. . . Eleven seconds . . . ten . . . nine . . . eight . . .

"Shoot!" yelled a White Cats fan. "Shoot, Johnny!"

. . . Seven seconds . . . six . . . five . . .

Johnny broke past Butch, felt Butch's hand slide across his shoulders. He leaped and laid the ball against the boards. In!

The crowd went wild.

The Red Foxes took out the ball. A player shot a long one as the clock ticked off the last second. The ball struck the rim, bounced off. The game was over. The White Cats won, 63 to 62.

Johnny was happy but not completely satisfied. When he got home he checked over the schedule. The next game against the Hornets was on January 18, the last game of the season for both teams.

The White Cats trimmed the Leopards on Thursday, and lost by a wide margin, 68 to 52, on Tuesday to the Swordtails, who were leading the league. On the thirteenth the White Cats beat the Astro Jets, 57 to 49.

At last came the game with the Hornets. Among the fans that filled the stands were Mom and Dad, Grandpa, and, of course, Mr. Sain.

Johnny started, playing opposite Jim. Both grinned at each other as they shook hands. Then the grins disappeared. They were opponents again.

The ball went up between the centers. Rick tapped it to Johnny. Jim tried to take it from him, but Johnny pivoted around on his right foot — doing it almost perfectly now —

then dribbled toward the Hornets basket. Jim dashed in front of him and Johnny passed to Toby in the corner. Toby shot. A hit!

The Hornets took out the ball and moved it swiftly upcourt. A pass to Jim. Johnny tried to intercept it, slipped, and fell. Jim broke for the White Cats basket. He leaped. A perfect layup.

Johnny got up and hustled downcourt. Cotton was bringing the ball down, dribbling cautiously, running slowly. Johnny trotted to the corner, circled in front of Jim. Cotton shot the ball to him. Johnny caught it and in one motion snapped a shot. The ball struck the rim, bounced high, and came down.

Johnny bolted in for the rebound. Alongside of him was Jim. They both leaped, their arms stretched high for the ball. Johnny put all the spring he could into his jump.

He soared higher. He got the ball! He came down with it, jumped again, and shot. A basket!

"Nice shot, Johnny!" he heard his father yell. Then Grandpa, too.

Johnny squirted upcourt, thinking about that jump. No one could call him "Lead-foot" now. Especially not Mr. Sain. He really didn't mind "Johnny Long Legs" anymore. As a matter of fact, "Johnny Long Legs" didn't sound bad at all.

The Cats led at the end of the quarter, 13 to 10. Johnny had sunk two for four points. In the next quarter he sank three, two layups and a corner shot. Toby dumped in two from a corner. Cotton was sinking them, too. They were hot.

The Hornets closed up the margin the first four minutes of the second half. Johnny came out, replaced by Stitch Buttons. Coach Dates gave all the members a chance to play, regardless of how far ahead or behind the White Cats were.

At the end of the third quarter the Cats led, 47 to 44. The Hornets were closing up the gap fast.

The game was an important one. If the Hornets won they would clinch second place and the White Cats would finish up in third. If the White Cats won the two teams would be tied for second. They would have to play off for second place. *We have to win,* thought Johnny.

The fourth quarter started with the White Cats taking out the ball. Johnny caught the throw-in from Toby and passed to Huck. Huck dribbled a bit. Suddenly a Hornet swooped in, swiped the ball from him, and dribbled all the way downcourt. Up and in. It was Jim Sain.

"Nice play, Jim!" yelled a familiar voice.

47 to 46.

Again Toby took out the ball. And again Johnny caught it and dribbled upcourt. Instantly Jim was after the ball and Johnny knew that from now on till the end of the game Jim was going to be one fast-moving, fighting basketball player.

Suddenly Jim got his hands on the ball. He tried desperately to yank it out of Johnny's hands but Johnny hung on.

Jump ball.

The ball went up. The boys leaped as high as they could. Again Johnny soared higher. He tapped the ball to Cotton. Cotton dribbled it upcourt and passed to Toby in the corner. Toby took a set and missed. Johnny, Rick, and Jim sprang for the rebound.

Again Johnny caught it. He leaped, arcing the ball. A basket! 49 to 46.

The fans were jubilant. "Come on, Johnny Long Legs!" shouted two familiar voices, Dad's and Grandpa's. "Sock it to 'em, boy!"

Johnny smiled.

The minutes ticked rapidly away. Both teams scored again and again. There was one minute left when Jim took a shot from near the center line and made it! 59 to 58, the Cats still leading.

The White Cats took out the ball and dribbled it carefully upcourt. Huck had it, passed to Johnny. Jim bolted in and tried to snatch it from him. Johnny pivoted away and broke for the basket. He shot. A miss!

He, Rick, and Jim went up for the rebound. Rick got it, shot, missed. This time Jim caught it and started to dribble away, but Johnny clamped his hand on the ball.

Jump ball.

Again Johnny outjumped Jim. Huck caught the tap and passed to Toby. A Hornet stole it from him, passed to another Hornet. The Hornet passed to Jim. Jim dribbled it hastily downcourt, Johnny after him. Johnny burst in between Jim and the basket and Jim stopped dead. He was in the keyhole. He shot. A hit.

Three seconds later the game was over. The Hornets won it, 60 to 59.

The Hornets swung their arms around each other, yelling and jumping happily. They yelled for the White Cats: "One! Two! Three! Hooray! White Cats!" Then they shook hands with the losers and ran down to the locker room. All except Jim, who was standing beside Johnny and Toby, watching their best-loved fans advancing toward them.

They all started to talk at once, shaking the boys' hands and saying how good a game it was.

"You really have come a long way, Johnny," said Mr. Sain, a happy glint in his eyes. He looked much different now than he had a couple of weeks ago. He had a new hat and his clothes were cleaned and pressed. "I remember when Jim outjumped you every time. Now you spring up past him like nobody's business. What did you do? Put wings on your feet?"

"I just practiced," replied Johnny, smiling.

"I want to apologize, Johnny," continued Mr. Sain in a quiet voice. "I'm sorry for calling you 'Leadfoot' and other silly names. You certainly aren't a leadfoot anymore. Anyway, I'm one of those fans who yell 'Kill the umpire!' at baseball games. I really don't mean anything by it."

"That's okay, Mr. Sain," said Johnny.

"Call him Johnny Long Legs," said Toby. "He doesn't mind that one bit anymore."

Everyone laughed.

Jim tapped Johnny on the shoulder. "Come on, Johnny Long Legs," he said, grinning. "Let's shower up and go home."

Matt Christopher

Terrell Davis

John Elway

Julie Foudy

Wayne Gretzky

Ken Griffey Jr.

Mia Hamm

Grant Hill

Derek Jeter

Randy Johnson

Michael Jordan

Lisa Leslie

Tara Lipinski

Mark McGwire

Greg Maddux

Hakeem Olajuwon

Briana Scurry

Sammy Sosa

Tiger Woods

Steve Young

The #1 Sports Series for Kids

Read them all!

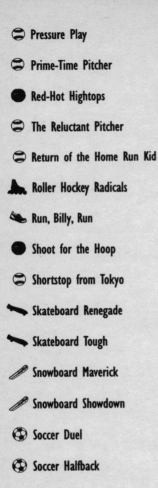
All available in paperback from Little, Brown and Company